Good children's literature appeals not only to the child in the adult, but also to the adult in the child.

– Anonymous

Second Edition 2010

Copyright 2004, 2010
Judith R. Vicary Swisher

Published by Rogers Press
Printed in Canada by Friesens Corporation

THE LAST ORNAMENT

Judith Vicary Swisher

Illustrations by Molly Mann

Christopher and Noelle
were so excited when it was
almost time for Christmas.

They had been very, very good –
well, maybe just very good – the
whole year long, and they knew
that Santa would be sure
to come to their house,
down the chimney.

Everyone had been so busy getting ready,
baking cookies and wrapping presents.

But the best part, of course, was their beautiful tree, which the whole family decorated a week before Christmas. First it was covered with tiny lights, then the decorations, dozens and dozens of them, each a special reminder of Christmases past.

There were bells
and toy animals, angels
and dolls, little flower
baskets and tiny stockings,
Santas from around the
world, clowns and cats,
hearts and reindeer,
and, of course, the
little Blue Engine.

One by one
they were carefully
unwrapped.
The children, and
Mommy and Daddy
too, had all picked
out their favorite
ornaments to
put on the tree.

Finally all the ornaments had been hung and the lights were turned on. Oh, how beautiful it looked, as the family admired their Christmas tree in the soft lights.

That's when the fun began for all the ornaments too. They had been packed away in their boxes since last year and now was their time to shine! They did what they had waited all year to do.

The little bells rang as they were hung on the tree, and then softly chimed with each slight breeze in the air. The toy soldiers stood straight and tall and proud, and the toy animals winked at the children.

The little blue engine was hung right beside the yellow elephant and they both smiled and smiled at everyone who passed by. The little red hearts shone with love, and the clowns danced a silly jig as the branches moved around them.

The ornaments even whispered to each other about how much fun they were having. Of course, they were careful that no one heard them.

But late at night, after everyone had gone to bed, a quiet visitor could have heard them proudly talking about how glad they were to be there, making everyone so happy.

On Christmas morning Noelle and Christopher had a wonderful time, opening their presents. Lots of family and friends came to visit and everyone admired the beautiful tree and all its many ornaments.

Christmas fun lasted for many days but finally it was time for the holidays to be over.

Even the ringing bells and the smiling elephant and the dancing clowns were getting tired.

The family gathered again, and lovingly packed the ornaments away until next December.

Then they carefully carried the empty tree out to the back porch.

Meanwhile the ornaments called out to each other in their box. "Is everyone here, and settled?" The clown asked, "Has anyone seen Blue Engine?" "No, no" came back a chorus of answers.

Oh dear, where could he be? Each ornament called to him and looked around in their tissue paper, but there was no Blue Engine. What had happened to him?

Out on the porch
where the old Christmas
tree lay in a heap of snow,
it was getting dark
and cold.

And nestled in a tangle
of branches there he was,
little Blue Engine. Somehow
he had been missed when
the ornaments were
taken off the tree and
packed away.

In all the piles
of tissue paper,
boxes and toys no
one had noticed. But
he noticed, especially
when it began to get
colder and colder,
and the snow
started to fall.

What could he do? He tried twirling around when the wind blew, and even tried to move his bright red smokestack around when a light went on above him on the porch.

But no one saw Blue Engine and came outside to rescue him. The family was soon sitting down to dinner together.

Meanwhile the ornaments were very worried inside their box and tried to think of some way they could get Daddy and Mommy's attention.

But the little bells couldn't ring, all wrapped up in tissue paper, and no one could see the twinkling stars who were trying so hard to shine brightly.

During dinner
Noelle and
Christopher
talked about all
their new toys
and the fun
they had
at Christmas.

And they both agreed
when Mommy and
Daddy said it had been
the most beautiful
Christmas tree they
ever had.

Christopher said he was sad to see the tree come down and asked if he could go look at it one more time. How silly his parents said, "It's cold and snowy outside and you'll get all wet."

"Please, please", he begged and finally the porch lights were turned on so they could all look out and admire the beautiful fir tree one last time.

As they stood looking at the tree, a slight breeze rustled through its branches, or was it a star winking in the sky?

Suddenly Noelle and Christopher saw the ornament and cried out together, "The little Blue Engine is still on the tree" as they ran to open the door.

Reaching into the
cold and snowy
branches Christopher
pulled out a very wet
and chilled Blue Engine
who was positively
shaking in the tree.

"That's one of our favorite ornaments", both children exclaimed as Noelle carefully dried him off. "It would have been so awful if we hadn't found him". The little Blue Engine agreed, although he couldn't tell them so.

After he was dry and warm they wrapped Blue
Engine in tissue and then lovingly put him back in
the box with all the other ornaments. As the
children went off to bed, the ornaments were
again happily together.

"We're so glad the children found you.
It just wouldn't be Christmas next year
if you weren't with us", they said.

The little Blue Engine agreed
and happily snuggled down in
the tissue with his friends.

And until the next time
they came out of their boxes
to be hung on the tree they
told the story again and again
about the Last Ornament, and
how wonderful it was that the
children found their little
Blue Engine.

Every year after that,
whenever a new ornament
was added to the family's
collection, Christopher and
Noelle remembered how
they had found the
Blue Engine.

They wished that every
family had children who
would search carefully
for the Last Ornament on
their own Christmas tree!

For Parents

Usually children are excited and
willing to help decorate the Christmas
tree. The challenge is to 'take down' the
tree after the holidays are over. Families can
turn it into a game, with the "Last Ornament"
challenge. The one who finds the almost-missed last
ornament is the winner and gets a special treat,
such as choosing the evening's dinner, or
being excused from a chore. But watch
out—a zealous helper sometimes can
hide one, and there might be
several 'almost last'
ornaments.

Have fun!

Judith Vicary Swisher